Fancy NANCY

and the Late, Late, LATE Night

Based on *Fancy Nancy* written by Jane O'Connor

Cover illustration by Robin Preiss Glasser

Interior illustrations by Carolyn Bracken

HARPER FESTIVAL
An Imprint of HarperCollinsPublishers

HarperFestival is an imprint of HarperCollins Publishers.

Fancy Nancy and the Late, Late, LATE Night
Text copyright © 2010 by Jane O'Connor
Illustrations copyright © 2010 by Robin Preiss Glasser

ISBN 978-0-06-201088-9

10 11 12 13 14 CWM 10 9 8 7 6 5 4 3 2 1

I adore visiting my neighbor Mrs. DeVine.
Here we are having tea on her veranda.
(That's a fancy word for porch.)

When she was a child, Mrs. DeVine lived in Hollywood. She used to see lots of movie stars—only Mrs. DeVine calls them celebrities.
Isn't that fancy?

She has a special scrapbook of photographs.
Some are autographed.
That means celebrities signed them.

"Your scrapbook is extremely fascinating," I say.
(Fascinating is even more interesting than interesting.)

Ooh la la! Mrs. DeVine says I can borrow her scrapbook if I bring it back tomorrow. "Merci, merci, merci!" I say.

At home I pretend that I am a Hollywood celebrity.
I dress up in my most glamorous attire—that's fancy for clothes.

I give my autograph to all my fans.

I pose for photographs.

"I am *late* for a glamorous Hollywood party," I tell my fans.
"*Au revoir!*"
(You say it like this: aw ruh-VWA. That's French for "good-bye.")

On my door I put up a sign that says
Do Not Disturb,
because celebrities need their privacy.
I want to look through Mrs. DeVine's scrapbook,
but I hear my dad calling us all to dinner.

After dinner I learn all my spelling words.
I am practically an expert at spelling.
Before I know it, Mom says, "Nancy, time for bed."
Oh no! I haven't had a second to look at the scrapbook.

I beg my mom to let me stay up later. But my mom says no. "It's a school night. Tomorrow is Friday. Tomorrow you can stay up later."

I put on my nightie and get in bed.

My parents kiss me good night.
"Sleep tight," they say.

But guess what! I am not going to sleep.
Under the covers, I have concealed—
that's fancy for hidden—
a flashlight and the scrapbook.

I stay up very late.
It is almost ten o'clock when I put away the scrapbook
and turn off my flashlight.
I bet even celebrities don't stay up this late!

The next morning, when my dad wakes me up,
I am exhausted. Exhausted is even worse than tired.

At recess, I am too exhausted to jump rope with Bree and my friends.

I miss three of the words on the spelling list.
My brain is exhausted, too.

After school, I return Mrs. DeVine's scrapbook.
She asks if I would like to stay for dinner
and watch a movie called *National Velvet*.

"It is on TV tonight. It is about a girl and a horse.
I loved it when I was your age," she says.
It sounds fascinating, but I can hardly keep my eyes open.

I go home and start weeping—which is fancy for crying.
When my dad asks what's wrong, I confess.
"I was naughty. I stayed up late last night and
I had a terrible and exhausting day."

My dad doesn't scold me. He says, "Now you understand why you need a good night's sleep."

That night I go to bed even earlier than my sister!

On Saturday I wake up feeling glorious again.
(Glorious is fancy for wonderful.)

And guess what—Mrs. DeVine taped the movie for me!
I can see it tonight.
Dad was right—even fancy girls need their beauty rest.

Alex turns and bows. "Merci, Nancy!"

When my parents come home
I tell them, "Alex is a sensational babysitter.
I hope he comes again soon."

I put cookies on a plate.
We drink lemonade out of teacups.
I remind Alex to keep his pinky up.
It is fancier that way.

Whew! We are both thirsty now.
We need refreshments.

Alex tries to hula.
He looks so funny!
Still, I try hard not to giggle because
that would be very rude.

"I can teach you," I say.
I demonstrate how to hula.
(Demonstrate is a fancy word for show.)
Not to brag, but I can hula
hoop for soooo long.

Then I show Alex my hula hoop.
"Wow! I always wanted to learn to do that,"
he says.

I try to juggle three—impossible!
Even two is very hard.
(If you don't believe me, try it yourself.)

We go downstairs.
Alex finds four tennis balls.

Ooh la la!
Alex is an expert at juggling.
He can keep four balls in the air.

"Wow! You got her to bed so early.
And she didn't even cry."
He asks if I want to learn to juggle.
 "Oui, oui, oui," I say.

I am reading a book to my doll Marabelle
when there is a knock on the door.
"*Entrez*," I say. (That's French for "come in.")
It is Alex.
"Your sister is asleep," he says.

Instead, I go upstairs to my room.
Alex can't help being a boy.
Still, seeing my agenda makes me a little melancholy,
which is fancy for sad.

My sister and Alex are building with her blocks.
Alex asks me to come play with them.

Oh no!
This is practically a babysitting tragedy.
But I try to be polite.
I hold out my hand and say, "Enchanté."
(That's French for "pleased to meet you.")

I am very confused. In fact, I am stupefied.
A teenager is in our living room—a boy teenager.
"Where is Alex?" I ask.
"I'm Alex," he says.

Soon I hear my mom calling,
"Come meet Alex."
I run downstairs.

First we'll play with my dolls.
Then we can play dress up.
Or maybe Alex will bring some fashion magazines.
We can look through them and pick our favorite ensembles.
(That's a fancy word for outfits.)

I make an agenda for the evening's activities.
An agenda is like a list, only fancier.
This evening will be so enjoyable—that's fancy for fun.

I help my sister get into her pj's.
I hope she goes to sleep early.
Then Alex and I will have lots of time together.

Tonight our parents are going to the movies.
A new babysitter is coming.
Her name is Alex and she is a teenager.
I am very excited.

HarperFestival is an imprint of HarperCollins Publishers.

Fancy Nancy and the Sensational Babysitter
Text copyright © 2010 by Jane O'Connor
Illustrations copyright © 2010 by Robin Preiss Glasser

ISBN 978-0-06-201088-9

10 11 12 13 14 CWM 10 9 8 7 6 5 4 3 2 1

Fancy NANCY and the Sensational Babysitter

Based on *Fancy Nancy* written by Jane O'Connor
Cover illustration by Robin Preiss Glasser
Interior illustrations by Aleksey and Olga Ivanov

HARPER FESTIVAL
An Imprint of HarperCollins*Publishers*